PRAISE FOR RE: WILD HER

"Webb-Campbell's nomad-like grazing on the treasures and pleasures of the world is sensuous, hungry, restless; the throat of this poet is wide open, expectant. In swallowing life and earth's marvels, she herself becomes them, and encourages the same of her reader."
—Shani Mootoo, author of *Oh Witness Dey!*

"These poems are wanderers, boldly straying across the globe (France, Cypress, Mexico, Cuba, California, Newfoundland) and in and out of the past, unafraid of 'strange creature sightings'—seeking them, in fact. They are poems hungry for magic and eager for transport, harkening to Elders and Buddhists, astrology and transatlantic flights, Two-Eyed Seeing and tarot. The transport sought isn't the sort that offers escape from the world but one that pushes past the dominance of Enlightenment-style reason and opens a person up to mutuality and wonder."
—Sue Sinclair, author of *Almost Beauty: New and Selected Poems*

PRAISE FOR LUNAR TIDES

Finalist for the 2022 Foreword INDIES Award for Poetry
Longlisted for the 2023 Fred Cogswell Award for Excellence in Poetry

"*Lunar Tides* is a poetry collection that I would recommend to readers looking to explore the meaning of grief and grieving or to those who want a better understanding of how the moon cycles influence us in our daily lives."
—Kaylie Seed, *Cloud Lake Literary*

"What rises above everything else in this collection of poems is the deep love that is woven into all of the poems. How does a daughter remember and mark her mother's life? Webb-Campbell does this beautifully in *Lunar Tides*, not flinching or avoiding death or loss."
—Kim Fahner, *periodicities*

T0343631

"Webb-Campbell explores the idea of 'mother' as meta-origin birthplace/home and also the literal mother of the poems' speaker, who is grieving her own mother's death."
—Angela María Spring, *Washington Independent Review of Books*

"The structure of the collection, following as it does the waxing and waning of the moon, the ebbing and flowing of the tide, both reinforces the ongoing harm of colonial and capitalist ways of thinking, ways that insist on a tidy and timely resolution of grief and, later in the collection, assembles an alternative vision: 'Learn that loss has its own time, and you are a small animal reeling.'"
—Melanie Brannagan Frederiksen, *Winnipeg Free Press*

PRAISE FOR I AM A BODY OF LAND

Finalist for the 2019 A.M. Klein Prize for Poetry

"*I Am a Body of Land* blends poetics, politics, criticism, and ethics without diminishing the affective beauty of poetry and its ability to speak to the reader's soul."
—Jessica Janssen, *Canadian Literature*

"Shannon Webb-Campbell searches, and talks to us about her search through her poems. Full of feelings, hardship and some joy. This engaging collection of poems is sometimes dark and sometimes gives us hope but not without reminders that we need to work for it."
—A.M. Klein Prize for Poetry jury citation

"Poetry awake with the winds from the Four Directions, poetry that crosses borders, margins, treaties, yellow tape warning: Police Line. Do Not Cross. Poetry whose traditional territory, through colonization, has become trauma and shame. Unceded poetry. Read. Respect. Weep."
—Susan Musgrave, author of *Exculpatory Lilies*

RE: WILD HER

SHANNON WEBB-CAMPBELL

Book*hug Press
Toronto 2025

Library and Archives Canada Cataloguing in Publication

Title: Re: wild her / Shannon Webb-Campbell.
Names: Webb-Campbell, Shannon, 1983– author.
Identifiers: Canadiana (print) 20240524195 | Canadiana (ebook) 20240526252
  ISBN 9781771669337 (softcover)
  ISBN 9781771669344 (EPUB)
Subjects: LCGFT: Poetry.
Classification: LCC PS8645.E225 R4 2025 | DDC C811/.6—dc23

The production of this book was made possible through the generous assistance of the Canada Council for the Arts and the Ontario Arts Council. Book*hug Press also acknowledges the support of the Government of Canada through the Canada Book Fund and the Government of Ontario through the Ontario Book Publishing Tax Credit and the Ontario Book Fund.

Book*hug Press acknowledges that the land on which we operate is the traditional territory of many nations, including the Mississaugas of the Credit, the Anishnabeg, the Chippewa, the Haudenosaunee, and the Wendat peoples. We recognize the enduring presence of many diverse First Nations, Inuit, and Métis peoples, and are grateful for the opportunity to meet and work on this territory.

For the wild ones,
ruled by winds, water, and beauty

"I do not believe in time I do believe in water."
—Dionne Brand

"A man can't live without a moral code. Mine is that I'm against the burning of witches. Whenever they burn a witch I get all hot under the collar."
—F. Scott Fitzgerald

"For the wild witches that no man (and no system) could ever begin to contain."
—Cherie Dimaline

re·wild
/rē•wīld/
verb
1. restore (an area of land) to its natural uncultivated state (used especially with reference to the reintroduction of species of wild animals that have been driven out or exterminated).

her
/hər,(h)ər/
pronoun
1. used as the object of a verb or preposition to refer to a female person or animal previously mentioned or easily identified.

CONTENTS

WILD-LIFE

CONNECTIONS

RECOVERY

WILD-LIFE

HER EROS RESTORED

after Gérard Deschamps *Les Chiffons de La Châtre—Corsets roses*, printemps 1960

*

on the last day of summer
a transatlantic flight over midnight
catapults us through moonlight
before a swirling hurricane
touches land on the Equinox
we kick up a fuss
as la Ville Lumière embraces
its second new year

*

at Le Comptoir Parisen alone
I write long after Anaïs Nin
for a world that does not exist
she was the first of her kind
to pursue sexuality and pleasure for its own sake
I am now a sultry femme
a visionary sprite
who splits, sips, and swills

*

we are drinking champagne with the rats
on the steps of the Pantheon
beneath the only star
you toast to the writers and philosophers
with brut out of paper cups
I thank the poets, chemists, and revolutionaries
blood buzzed we tiptoe backward
separately along the Seine

*

I need to break the glass of Deschamps's
Les Chiffons de La Châtre—Corsets roses
smash the patriarchy
set women's rags and underwear free—
it's no longer springtime in the 1960s, ladies!
unhinge your brasseries, panties, corsets, and girdles
let the old girls breathe and fight back
wives, mothers, child-eaters, witches, and whores

*

you see the lights
illuminate Palais Garnier
I am strapped inside the opera house
on a boat ride of toil-and-trouble woes
charting a three sisters' tragedy
waves of love, lust, and revenge
while fancy Parisians take candlelit selfies
you wander solo in hurricane rain

*

after the wages of crude men
who cornered on slick streets
with too-aggressive tongues
pushed me hard down cobblestone
I became a Paris runaround
wearing extravagant outfits—
pleather dresses, pleated skirts, quixotic feathers
you restored my best lace

*

reading E. E. Cummings's *erotic poems* out loud
under covers we tangle like root vegetables
wrapped up in borrowed sheets *around you*
and forever: I am the hugging sea
tracing my lips with your wet fingertips
you tell me you only desire
to draw me nude—
but you never do

HOOKING A STORM'S EYE

you had to gnaw on
seaweed-laced secrets
toxic periwinkle dramas

outstrip ancestral trauma
retreat to unfamiliar shores
and leave lights on

what raged in your cell walls?

three years ago
dawn cried forth
our new cosmology

earthbound you left
hooked a journey
through the storm's eye

historically, mother
we go way back
refashion visionary time

was I once your mother?

somehow you are
light years everywhere
yet nowhere I can grasp

you meet earthbound edges
ascend like eagles
sleep with fish

what am I most grateful for?

your soothing calls
all these battling years
a voice I can't let go of

humming night meditations
your introspective lullabies
temper my agitation

your quietude surrounds
my bedrock of brooding
creates a reckoning calm

you clawed your way
without a sanctum
to feel our cove embrace

OSTARA

welcoming the sun's entry into Aries
casting ourselves chakra deep
awaiting our seasonal shift
we kick up our bare heels
to smell earth's rapture

we are marking light's victory
new rituals to measure day for night
slowly spinning to vinyl in the parlour room
me dressed as a goddess
and you in your best suit and tie

you bend to kiss my crystals while I hold your runes

SIRENS OFF CAPRI

making love Calypso deep
in the underwater cavity

I become half fishwoman
flopping with Parthenope
who birthed the Isle of Sirens
flying over ospreys

a watery land-shaped female body
stretches out in the blue glow
where nymphs crawled over
to become rocks, hardened

where high waves slam fish tails against caverns
in the dark of Grotta Azzurra
who try to escape a father-son mythology
centuries of pain open

the low cave mouths

COSMIC WOODLAND GUIDANCE

you came to me as a valley
dreamlike in your twenties
vixen of the hunt
moon spells and birthing
begged me to let go
gather my skirts
dying is not the end
seven generations rallied
you lived out every little onslaught
now you're a new woman
wilder than motherhood

TRANSATLANTIQUE

I want to become Transatlantique
drape my spirit in Barbier costume
tango between Halifax and Paris
flow in elaborate gowns
held up by whalebone corsets
dance with the crème de la crème
my iridescent peacock feathers
swirl with womankind
rebellious godmothers who crossed the grey ocean
by steamer seeking new life
who broke traditions
to hang Parisian doors in their kitchen
spending their years living in surrealist motifs

TAROT DE LA LUMIÈRE

before fortune-telling
we trusted the history
structured by tarot

planetarily spinning
a search for divinations
self-reflected in Google's orbit

in studio I pull a trinity
from a French deck
calling on the Tarot of Light

Roi de Denier
Reine de Denier
Cinq de Coupe

King of Pentacles guides our past
Queen of Pentacles nurtures the present
Five of Cups teaches our future of impermanence

DEEP ECOLOGY

tree-planting a vast, brutal countryside
mountain visions reach sky
plants can't grow taller than tuckamore
we're doing well by surviving
there is no romance to desolation
this is a bleak wasteland

will you be my tender pine?
wrap me around your riverbank?

ecologists want to rewild
create au natural not seen for centuries
trees should grow:
pines, silver birch, rowan
did you know there are sacred seeds
nesting in you since before you were born?
don't attach to manifestation

let go of your fury to
acknowledge your needs

STARDUST WOMAN

when you roll with a stardust woman
Scorpion to the bone, you'll see comets throw
blazes across the blackest of night
a femme made of cooling gases from stars
who steals Veuve Clicquot from a capricious lover
pours you a flute, wearing metallic sequins
you drink dust grains blowing across space
she's no violent supernova, but you know
her ex-lover will be destroyed again
through decay she gifts
a packet of seedlings to plant after the thaw
muses about her grandmother who waltzed
down the aisle carrying a sprig of sweet peas

ERUPTING AURORA

the pilot flies into otherworldly skies
windborne over the tip of Labrador
erupting through aurora borealis
stars guide us over North Sea
light dancers streak across frozen tundra
dreamers sing out for the light show
as above with Greenland below
where a sunrise landing disrupts
a volcanic island punctuated by ice

DO NOT TOUCH THE MOSS

for many dark eons
lava fields were barren
until wind carried
spores from elsewhere

with over six hundred species
it takes hundreds of years
for tiny mosses to grow
woolly fringe

take a lesson from moss
one of our first settlers
does not claim ownership
only protects the land

ANOTHER TEMPORARY HOME

Lava. Volcanic ash. Half the year in darkness. The other half
in endless light.
A heaviness settles in. The lava-punctuated island lurks above
the globe. A swift leaving so no one will notice. A rupture,
a volcano. One day you are here. Another you are gone.
The government doesn't want anyone to know your
departure.
An envelope lands on your doorstep to tell you that you are
not, and never will be
an islander. As if you didn't already know that. You came on a
boat. You'll leave
on the wind. Less sudden than death, but another severed tie.
You never chose this
island. It will never choose you back. This place, that place—
there's no place for you.
Black lava becomes a memory. Stones from the black beach
nestle into the soles of your shoes. A Nordic darkness
covers. No sparks, or light to carry you.
Your body is shipped elsewhere. Another place that is not your
place.
Another temporary home that is not your home.
You know you can't go back, but you have no choice in where
you move forward.
Your body is not yours. Your spirit is salted.
Your liver is pickling. You'll never belong.
You need to get as far away as you can go.

SEASONAL WITCHES

when I look out my window
what do you think I see?

hanging over Greenwich Mean Time
sipping a tinned espresso martini, a mile high
why do you think the green witch was mean?

must be the vinyl ruby slippers
displayed in a flea market's aperture below
you never wanted to be a bad witch from the west

you aligned with Glinda's potions
but these days you don't make sharp distinctions
you know bitches brew all kinds of anthems
grooving to *season of the witch*

OFF ISLA MUJERES (BAY OF WOMEN)

sirens call out for Ixchel
across the island of women
her power ripples
where the Caribbean Sea
licks the Gulf of Mexico

kindreds comb beaches
for relics of fertility
swim in medicinal waters
before the Mayan moon goddess
we offer our feminine forms

Ixchel interweaves textiles
impregnates us with salty potions
as lizards haven upon her rocks
sea turtles defend her shores
we listen to her holler

CARGO

on an old wartime bunker
a house looks off toward Europe
shelters the brutal hours
at the mouth of Kjipuktuk
witnesses transatlantic cargo
ships arriving from distant places

lulled by rolling waves
pull the house up from under
your boathouse lines horizon
soothed by the night
only to deny visions
of unbelonging

DARK YEARS OFFSHORE

I've come for seaweed
to weave kelp-laced anklets
swimming in cyan

my morning dip
a waterbed reverie
rarifies ice bath plunges

whispering *I'm here*
a flock of pelicans' choir
schools of tropical minnow pipe in

my selkie tail sways
in an oceanic hammock
welcomes an ethos of forgiveness

PLANT-SITTING AT SEA

trying not to overwater succulents
in the living room I mistake
plants for people
who bend for light

in this boredom I see how starfish
connect like salt and pepper shakers
at the kitchen sink I twirl the propeller
of a small toy airplane

take me anywhere
but here
away from this body
away from my skin

I've tried bowing before Buddha
I winked at the miniature owl
but nothing turns the hourglass over
like a one-eyed aluminum fish

off the back deck I feel sunlight
catch a flock of paper cranes soaring
beneath my feet a shoreline gathers
skyward through moving clouds
shimmering off the seawater

I ditch the plane
boomerang a starfish
and dive headfirst
into the glitter

SIPPING DEATH IN THE AFTERNOON

nothing stirs the imaginary
like drinking anise flavours

a masquerade of green fairies
dance in coupes laced with dry bubbles

breathing in wormwood
a moody jigger of absinthe

trills of the underworld
topped by chilled champagne

there's no need to shake
death in the afternoon

you'll acquire opalescent milkiness
lost in strange realms

find yourself in shadows
where effervescence concoctions whisk

windy night ripples off
one of Hemingway's cocktails

the author recommends
drink three to five of these slowly

tells you if you place a photo of human ashes
under a microscope you will see we are stars

MOONRAKER LIVES FOREVER

burning off the years amongst century flora
foxtail agaves, succulents, and prickly pears
the fire danger index along Sea Ranch
rates these days as low potential

when I heard Nova was blazing
I was swimming off Moonraker
a geothermal pool tucked into the land
where native plants live forever

climate changes outlooks, coastlines, and fauna
somewhere off foggy California wild turkeys run
fawns follow does through long grasses
we're seeking moonsail in hopes
to shelter our old growth

WITCHES' KEY

I didn't fall for spells
of Cayo Las Brujas
a Cuban island of sea women
where wooded evergreen
meets shrubs and thickets
off Jardines del Rey

I am not afraid of
strange creature sightings
ghosts of old lovers
ivory-coloured sands
karst cliffs over mangroves
wallowing in brackish water

I know cut-off
worn-away terrain
seabed typography
how erosion unlocks
dissolves soluble rocks
hexes turn this witches' key

CONNECTIONS

IN THE MIDST OF A CITY CRY

you came upon an amphitheatre
where Mi'kmaw feasted on St. Aspinquid's Day
burial grounds where two chiefs fought during the war
only to stand alone punching up the sky
a fist fight between your internal divides

you go wandering beyond
a blue-collared dockyard
toward a pointed coastal park
you smell pine, touch rust
sense ancestor trees

you're leaning out your portal
to watch a branch dance
trying to grasp weather patterns
practise urban forest bathing
in a winter storm surge

looking out to the Atlantic, gawking
you wonder how to begin again—
should I wrap myself around Glasgow lampposts?
lay my bloated body down
outside a chapel made of stone?

ORBITING THE FOOL'S WHEEL

in heels, you cross your legs

face heaven-line wearing red lipstick

swing lace-like circular motions

wearing your Sunday best

you ascend toward the horizon

float above sand dunes

drift below the universe

climbing the ladder

you look at your hands that hold centuries

learning to read palmistry

touch your own fingertips

place hands over your

                              throat chakra

            to feel light unbox from within

                        your inner mountain lion

        cascades across fleshy skies

                          deep into the cosmic blur

    you awaken a fiery comet

PINK UP PARCHED EARTH

rustic delicacies formed by soft hands
textured mosses become abstract vessels
pink and white earthen echoes
biological formations
waterlogged bark where barnacles grow
reshape stone's breath

you harness jagged cliffs
dig up frosted forest
foggy lichen under your fingernails
rocks peeling back the ocean floor
a deep philosophy of wabi-sabi
shallows in the tidal pools of your palms

water rushes over cracked earth
you retrace tides through clay
grounding mud with reversing rhythms
you see nature's aerial view minds algae
an organic process surfaces

what flows in
must flow out

OAPIMGOEEGAAMOGOAASI GISPASIG MAGEMIGEO

motalamoonog ola oelteg nogtagel opitenn gisitog

pasegangitasoagen tepagenn taan teltag pisagenn

oapimgoeeg ag oapeeg magimgeo togentaag

taan gôgoei mimatjig eliisig

masgoi sampoagoanig taan etligoeg agsgitoltitjig

iliamaligit gonteo taan oetlamit

giil gelpilmen oaleneegel taan mistonag

molgoat nepogt

eoneeg mesagenagel lameeg egtloigeng

gontal nisoogoael sitemoog

oetjitoon gelolg emset gôgoei

malpaag taan oesoegao egl amipten

gesigaoitg samgoan ola pasgaasig magemigeo

epgao eoemen goilmen oesoegao

mateemen sisgoo eoemen amaltaag apetjaasig

geneg oetaptemen magemigeo ôgotagemo angitaasoagenn

na ola taan gôgoei mimatjig igaag

taan gôgoei pisgoitg

na amotj teoitg

—translation of "Pink Up Parched Earth" by Joan Milliea

IMBOLC FERTILITY

a triple deity rebirths
halfway through winter
heralding a change of light—
a division between
solstice and equinox seeds
in the belly of my dead mother
I want to crawl back inside of

NOTES TO LUNA

how can I lift you up?
within these rituals of living
smaller schemes ache
my skeletal longs

I'm missing curves of you
in the veins of my dreams
come back so I can hear you purr
as our hunger upturns

ON THE LONGEST NIGHT

the solstice queen calls a wild hunt
from her throne of woodland greenery
decked-out winter pagans
sit with elements to greet
a procession of spirits
nightriders who seek blessings
a cacophony of geese, owls
old crows who cry out
toward the rebirthing sun

DEER PAST SELVES

how could you know

who you'd become

folded through time?

you smelled gun smoke

flax-woven seas of illusion

pain obscures desire

your energetic angst morphed

moonflowers into new visions

you dusted off the external jabber

finally picked your truest self

what did you see through?

who will you bubble into?

HIDE DOLL FILLETS

at the tip of Cabot Tower
you trace pink lady's slipper across
the narrows of St. John's
reaching toward the night

calling on your spirits
who wait in the shadows
bathing in shallows
offer candle invitations

your body cuts a hide fish-doll
laid thin on the port city's floor
concrete grasps her celestial spheres
confessions of a sea-laced finned leather girl

CAN I WRITE MY WAY INTO BELONGING?

transcend sunlight into sugar
energy creates new life
an alchemy of protein
kinship illuminates
chosen and biological family
affinity magnifies relational
stamens produce wings
like my grandmother's hands
in this house of exile

STARRY-EYED GAZES

our naked eye sees ten thousand stars
only a few are given names
astronomy groups asterisms
don't believe in individual stars

you cry my name across cosmos
island draws on the power of sea
rising watery energy bears clarity
your wave calls

what if my root system is stars?
my violet crown Antares swings
seven chakras run along my spine
this third eye opens like Canopus

my blue throat named Castor
awakens an ancient energy
blocked green like my heart Pollux
no wonder I can't speak or feel

what if bloodlines are hot gas?
open Rigel's yellow solar plexus
my orange sacral chakra Spica knows
Vega's roots grow way down

I MET A MAN NAMED JESUS

whose almond eyes twinkled like my father's
when he asked me to go to the disco

I told him I can't dance with the dead
he whispered in my ear in Español

something about how in Mexico they honour
ancestors by dancing with them

he offered his hand—
the dead come back, let's dance!

SHORELINES

rusty reds run through
a coal miner's daughter
born from metallic iron oxides
deep mineral veins
laced by the underground
two thousand feet below water's desires
black lungs took her father
she now bumps into the imaginary
cries out for shorelines that made her

LAGOON SKIES

under a thin veil of all-nights and no sleep
you wade through blue waterways
nestled between two shoulder cliffs
you mistake yourself for the sea
clouds part to help you awaken
a ritual reminds you are hot ash
realms of sky lagoons
a saltwater being
as you float, locals report
a nearby volcano could blow

PAPER PLAIN

looking out to the blues
glitter on the water
paper cranes fly
skyward through the clouds
what happens when you
stop seeing the magic
within the world
or in one another?

MY MOON, MY MAN

I want to become heavy
as a heart-shaped box filled
with ancient crystals
munching on hematite
you drift upward ingesting
delectable cosmology

you sail toward moon rays
hitching a ride on a paper lantern
a single flame
carries us over clouds
we float along
bite one another

OUT AT THE PARCELLES

muses are at the window
tapping on the glass
flushed with energy
they want to be invited
for a glass of something juicy

their bright eyes aglow
holding fans in their right hands
that cover half their faces
whispering *follow us*
into the night

geisha cheeks like cherries
they wave fans close to their hearts
you will have a stylish grave adorned
with pale reddish Victorian bouquets

THE SUBLIME WINKS

who does *she think she* is winking at the universe?
queering wonder she blooms spreading seedlings
tangled roots of kinship coalesce

IF I WERE A LOTUS

I'd spread silver white, sparsely hairy
short-stalked with a few leaves

though I'd rather be astragalus
heads turning, flushed by pink and purple flowers

but I'm a black locust with spiny stems
pale foliage drooping clusters of sweetness

a native tree widely planted on the Mediterranean

THE FUTURE IS BOTANIC

off the Thames
a prehistoric South African
palm tree has been living
for over two centuries

growing inch by inch
year by year where Woolf's short story
questions marriages and flower beds
a literary allusion

climbs the Victorian spiral staircase
to reach the hull of Kew's ship roof
a state of the art now in disrepair
to peek at the Eastern Cape cycad

dizzy from height's oasis heat
in the steamy Noah's Ark
for endangered species—
vines run up the steelwork

plants that never blossomed
began to open and grow wild
shattering panes of glass
in the palm house built in 1844

rising to meet a tip of the tropics
silver-blue Madagascar palm
rare island species
a different thorny perspective

in the living laboratory
of trembling orchids, exotics
live in a glasshouse rainforest
studied and protected by scientists for years

never once thought to be ripped from their roots
the future is botanic

RECOVERY

HOW DO I REACH FOR THE WILD?

(THREE GRACES)

ONE: GIRL

*

I cycle like hibiscus
open in the early morning
need unexpected radiance
trumpet and bloom
then wilt by day's end

*

how do I reach for the wild?
circle the womb
how can I grasp the wind?
motherlines ring a cosmic spin

*

what does it mean to return?
I want out of this rotunda
when did I become cultivated?
a point of great fragility erodes

*

was it at the time of my birth?
I entered a third state of being
when does water break?
revive pathbreaking liquids

*

I want to stop running away
New York streets undo
modern conditioning
skyward home

*

get off this carousel
a circular standstill
recalibrate to recreate
live beyond the domestic

*

I must unlock from grief—
align with Venus
ask Stein
where can I find
the woman in the waves

*

who told me we're all gods born from sea?
Aphrodite in wilful surrender
a siren, a whistling jar
in her age of decadence

*

she asked for three graces:
can you rewild an ecosystem?
is rewilding possible?
how did rewilding begin?

TWO: WOMAN

*

domesticity has got us down
this creature needs rewilding
disregard her original habitat
unlearn extraction

*

I ought to sing soothing R&B
like the security guard at the MoMA
who cultivates ecological restoration
steps away from the emphasis on humans

*

let's belt it out au natural
give melody to shape land and sea
doctors are prescribing National Parks passes
depressed patients need forest baths and ecotherapy

*

1, 2, 3, let's fertilize connection!
serve the summer
beyond displacement
remember you are wilderness

*

I can feel the purring of
mother and grandmother
on the wind
ahhhh, Leo season!

*

keep what's rooted in the ground
make sure to water your soles
I never cared about driftwood
until I understood death cycles

*

wellness industries sell
our bathtubs back to us
sea salt in jars costs
the same as gas

*

I need to rewild myself
stop collecting glassware
give up fluffing my grief cushions
to reach out in strange ways

*

I set the table
in the centre of the woods
attempt to embrace a bit of chaos
call out to the maples

THREE: CRONE

relinquish the reins
breathe a natural process
re-establish disorder
allow nature to take care of me

I reintroduce a species
regenerate hazel, hawthorn, and oak
rewild back
a self almost disappeared

I want to be whirling glass
a wild weed
I need to hairstreak a butterfly
squeeze floral diversity

*

despite our best rewilding efforts
without a fluke
truth undertakes the patriarchal mind
I see Plath at the window

*

why am I performing this domesticity?
who actually cares what the sheets are made from
anyone care about biodiversity?
I've lost faith in the concept of curation

*

I'm a poet
a woman
a motherless daughter
a lover
no one

*

I'm not married to a man
he's married to my coven
I miss my mother's disobedience
her ability to subvert social norms

*

the cold dippers have gone ice bathing
all winter long
cracking ice floes to open water
they grow cranky as the ocean-keeper warms

*

lakes and rivers rise
attract other bodies
private wilds
shivering electric

*

here we cut lupins to place them in glass jars
my grandmother thought flowers were a waste
how else can we bring a sense of the wild into ourselves?

*

my nan caught her own cod
I pay over twenty bucks a pop
at least it's not from a box
packaged to be sold as wild

*

the women wanted rooms
then they felt confined
later they wanted tides
and to fillet their own fish

*

while the city sought skyscrapers
the women looked for a home
we wanted out from our mother's thumb
beyond an elderly woman's kitchen

volume up tickets to the stars
play records to kiss strangers
sing your lungs out
dream of the uprising

*

become a fish-woman
emerge from the waters' offering
after a trinity of swims all in one day
baptism by sea

WILD HORSES RUN

sure-footed on a crescent-shaped isle
protected by a windswept past
colliding with the reeling present
digging my heels into an animistic future
adaptation becomes survival

fog rolls change, marvel at us animals
who thrive in harsh remote places
feral ponies in the far-flung North Atlantic
divvy up a breeding colony with grey seals
hundreds of playmates wash ashore
become their own archipelago

pups birthed in a sand-dune nursery
kin who call this fable key home

IF YOU ALIGN

she'll bring you Jupiter cakes
talk of your organs being like constellations
your liver is a planet orbiting
with potions of herbal knowledge

a boreal witch with a backstory explores
the forest of lost symbols
asks you to look up the word nature
most cultures don't skywrite wilderness

birth chart blueprints mark
a sacred marriage of the esoteric
she'll wait for you *at the powwow*
at the potluck to rewrite history

secret elixirs of light
chakras align
blood spirit moves
through your garden

SALT CURES

under the spell of rooibos

rock queens roar through the twenty-first century

belting out feminist incantations

pushing up bile in their throats unbridle visions of equality

salt blends of old herbs with new growth

to create the rites of a Victorian modernist

unlike the ever-entrancing lion's mane jellyfish

these contemporary rituals of verse chorus verse

combat the dark energies of patriarchy's persecution

feminism recoils in the blood

resilience develops in the body

divine femininity rug-hooks beauty

female empowerment

upends

the status quo

we will brine

DOGMA OF THE TIMES

nature's hostility is indifferent
to text messages
the urgency of now
healing mantras from bots
TikTok interruptions
chart your fitness progress
heart rate, ovulation, and dry days

esoterica works against
authoritarian regimes
remakes elemental myth
transgresses across epochs
impulsive truth-seekers
pivot as creativity purifies

libraries are rebellion
at ease with the unknown

A NEW YEAR HINGES

on the spectral solstice
threshold of day
claws back night
softness divines
releases her grip

be the seal who sun-worships
belly up flaked out on a rock

NEPTUNE WAKES UP

between the clearing years
floats avant-garde ways of being

double male and female
ancients seek polarity

to conjure south nodes
brushstrokes of lifetimes

sprinkle three-dimensional sunspots
direct links to stressors on the body

beauty marks tip off

you inherited a curious flow

TAKE ME TO THE PINK LAKES

strip off my tropical gothic dress
lay my decaying body on white sand
roll it over into crimson water
beneath pastel blue skies
let pale red salts carry me
until my skin dissolves
rosy like flamingoes
whose pigment becomes
feathery shades of Las Coloradas
rose from brine shrimp
a diet of plankton
fiery algae

under salmon-pink forbidden waters
watch my spirit swim
become blush

SEAWATER PORTALS

a meteor struck Yucatán
opening enigmatic tranquil water
natural pits from limestone bedrock
deep root veins tangle above
millions of years old cenotes

sinkholes with snapping turtles
scorpions, exotic fruit, and agave
a womblike cave for healing
once ancient Mayan bathing rituals
a portal between the living and the dead

now little catfish suck on your toes

A COVE IS A COVEN

out at the outport
looking back at the wharf
where we live
I see dockyards
a pointed park where I run
to look off to sea
a shoreline guides
my broken heart
through every storm
if I squint, I can see land
my isles call out for me
for now; I shelter in this bay
clutch my temporary coven

HEALING FORMS

I wandered into Lóla Flórens
an unorthodox café of old medicines
blooming herbal tea in glass coupes

a vintage shop meets champagne bar
sparkling wine, tarts, and tarot decks
I sat down to pull three cards

are your dreams luminescent
enough to keep you going
when things grow dark?

do they light the day when
you forget you wanted them?

the day after Beltane in Reykjavik
perched beyond rationale
stinking corpse lily blossomed strangely
an invitation to esoteric wisdom

a round table of shuffling spaces
I placed the cards back into the deck
to listen to women speak Icelandic

GEYSER

gathered in the muddy hot belly
deep water thousands of feet below
connects grandfather rocks that steam
hydrogeological fields meet magma
creating a hydrothermal explosion
of intense heat, water, and spray
land gushes orgasmic

I DIDN'T GO TO THE BLUE LAGOON

between two eclipses I fell unwell
too sick to lavish my body in muddy murk
mystical promises of youthful rejuvenation

instead I stayed in bed all day coughing
drinking tinctures, sucking on throat drops
sweating out toxins under wool blankets

at the airport I bought expensive black salt
after slathering my face in a sample algae mask
unpacked Blue Lagoon from an architect's perspective

a tourist trap rebranded as a worldly wonder
where thousands soak in geothermal overflow
waste from a power plant marketed as mineral waters

NEVER TURN YOUR BACK ON THE OCEAN

wandering raw and rugged cliffs
off Northern California
bowing down to fireweed

your eyes meet a cautionary sign
never turn your back on the ocean
could this be an omen?

nature's manifesto is smart-mouthed
you can't own bodies anyway
fools who try to suspend and drown

wild swimmers, cold dippers
salt revivalists
rebirth celestial bodies

TENDER WAS THE NIGHT

So, what if "Once upon a time" is fashioned in stone?
I walk under le Château de La Napoule's archway
mutter—*doesn't mean fairy tales come to life*
over late dinners in a gothic dining room

an exquisite young painter reflects
you look like you were born here
I'm shedding dead skins, I tell her
no longer noir and caustic

after spending starlit nights
on terraces overlooking Côte d'Azur
sipping from midnight's apothecary
wild gin palace botanicals

recalling I lived here in another era
a time when tragedy backlit beauty
dark affairs, secrets, and corruption
tarnished the French Riviera

tonight, we wait up for a hundred years
to see the lovers wake and reunite
in their keyless apartment floating up
from the tower above their tombs

SEVERE MOON RISES

draw on *carte da trionfi*
pull the triumph womb card
pathways grow
unfurl your root system

a three-card spreads swords
your past fans wands
your present challenges pentacles
your future directs cups

water trumps lunar shades
yawning layers into blue
a double-crested cormorant
lips over shoreline

STILL CALLING OUT JOEY

a man called Smallwood
decades after we became
so-called Canadians
reshaped identity
our land across the water
now we're being
uprooted in court
called out online
pretendians
wannabe Mi'kmaq
left to burn one another

CEREMONY COLLABORATION

late summer between islands
wild grasses on the wind
shorelines of rosa rugosa at low tide
at this time of ecological crisis
look to Elders and Buddhists
wildflowers who know meditation
the season shifts so we bend
pluck rose haw from bush
boil for rosehip soup
sea sage lingers on my nose
wafts of burning sweetgrass
helping recall tidal time
you find npisun within

NITAP

you are made of rocky earth
run steadily through seasons
gather strength in the woods

sun-sharp
wake before first light
honour each day

you remind me I'm made of wind
wild like a partridgeberry
born of moose calls

in our kinship conversations
your voice fills me with *island*
a dialect that calls me back

GENERATIONS MEET IN EPWIKEK

in No'kmaq Village we'll gather
where wilderness comes face to face with water
Flat Bay rivers on the east
Fischells on the west
ancestors left instructions to harvest
layers of deer foot fungus
latches on dying birch
count chaga rings five times from the bottom
to make a tea to stave off cancer
a sacred gift of Northern direction

LIVING AND DYING AMONGST THE TIDES

carrying rose quartz, tobacco, and dried flowers
my pockets lined with fox fur inside my winter coat
trying to keep warm sporting my Montréal beret
cold water, I need to speak with kitpu
I no longer know what belongs to the bay and what to my body

I can't afford the fifty-dollar antique *Book of Magic*
instead I walk dykeland to see Kjiku's moon rise
what brought me here and what have I lost?
I cry to the frozen land—I need to let go

look I'm back in the land of the living
here beauty is built on ruins

SWIMMING WITH THE ASHES

in the off-shoulder season
as autumn leaves undress
cedar at velvet chocolate lake

a gathering of mourners
hang their heads in prayer
on the shoreline holding petals

an old park bench philosophy:
new beginnings are often
disguised as painful endings

submerging my body
underwater I feel Kisu'lk
spirit returns to waves

your earthly remains
alight on sedimentary rocks
powdering the grandfathers

at the bottom of the lake
your ashes become fish food
speckles of spectacular ceremony

WATERMOTHER

it's always been East and West
a Cayman Trench between us

meet me in the subtropics of beauty
bring blood orange rinds, fried plantain

throughout the grey years
you've always been prismatic

in the blue-green sea
breaststrokes off a palm tree forest

gazing into the pink hazy horizon
we bellyflop to welcome new spirals

crawl out of the clamshell
will we become waves?

or will you pull the rolling sea
over my shoulders like a cape?

when do I become water, mother?

NOTES ON THE POEMS

"Her Eros Restored," is the recipient of the inaugural Ellemeno Visual Literature Prize 2024. Prize jurors had this to say: "'Her Eros Restored' loosens a too-tight corset—each of its poetic sections responding to *Les Chiffons de La Châtre—Corsets roses* [Rags of the Castle—Pink Corsets] (1960) by Gérard Deschamps. It does so by reclaiming small moments of feminine autonomy." Wela'lioq to prize jurors Sue MacLeod, Jessica Scott Kerrin, and Carol Shillibeer for this significant recognition, and to the Writers' Federation of Nova Scotia. This poem includes a line from the poem "as we lie side by side" by E. E. Cummings, from his book *Erotic Poems* (W. W. Norton & Company, 2010).

An earlier version of "Hooking a Storm's Eye" appeared in *Riddle Fence* Issue 47, March 2023.

"Transatlantique" is a poem that winks to *Transatlantique: The Art Deco of Fashion and Costume Design in Paris and Halifax*, an exhibition mounted at the Art Gallery of Nova Scotia and publication by Mora Dianne O'Neill and Arthur M. Smith (Art Gallery of Nova Scotia, 2018).

"Tarot de la Lumière" is inspired by a tarot deck found during my Canadian Artist Residence at Château de La Napoule, organized by La Napoule Art Foundation, Mandelieu-la-Napoule, Alpes-Maritimes, France, April 2024.

"Seasonal Witches" nods to Donovan's song "Season of the Witch" (1966).

"Sipping Death in the Afternoon," coined after Ernest Hemingway's nonfiction book, *Death in the Afternoon* (1932), is his cocktail invention of the same moniker—also known as the Hemingway, which is a mix of absinthe and champagne.

"Moonraker Lives Forever" is a poem inspired by the Sea Ranch, California's modernist utopia, a former sheep ranch on the Northern California coast in Sonoma County that was developed in the mid-1960s by architects Richard Whitaker, Donlyn Lyndon, Charles Moore, and William Turnbull Jr. *Moonraker* (1979) is also the title of a James Bond spy film.

"In the Midst of a City Cry" touches on elements found in Point Pleasant Park: a historic seventy-five-hectare woodland park on the south end of the Halifax peninsula in Mi'kma'ki.

"Pink Up Parched Earth" is an ekphrastic poem based on Darren Emenau's work *Scapra*, (earthenware, MNO lichen glaze, 21.5" x 9" x 9", 2019) and *Big Pink* (white earthenware, MNO lichen glaze, 8" x 17" x 8", 2019). This poem was created as part of the Atlantic Vernacular project, a digital exhibition curated by Craft NB in 2022. "Pink Up Parched Earth" was also translated into Mi'kmaw by Joan Milliea as part of this collaboration, and faces the original English poem in this book. Milliea's translation is titled "Oapimgoeegaamogoaasi Gispasig Magemigeo."

"My Moon My Man" is also the name of Feist's first single off of her album *The Reminder* (2007), which was co-written by Feist and Chilly Gonzales.

"Out at the Parcelles" came to me while I was on writing residency at The Parcelles Studio & Stay in Seaforth, Nova Scotia, Spring 2023.

"The Sublime Winks" is a poem inspired by Amy Ash's solo exhibition *Perennial Bodies* at the Beaverbrook Art Gallery in Spring 2023.

"The Future Is Botanic" references Virginia Woolf's short story "Kew Gardens," which was privately published in 1919 and more widely in 1921, and takes place in Kew Gardens in London, England. Kew is recorded in 1327 as cayho, and is a combination of two words: the Old French kai (landing place) and Old English hoh (spur of land), which is formed by the bend in the Thames.

"If You Align" references Joséphine Bacon narration in French and Innu from the exhibition *Indigenous Voices of Today* at the McCord Stewart Museum in Montréal, Quebec, in 2023.

An earlier version of "Salt Cures" appeared in *Riddle Fence* Issue 47, March 2023.

The poems "A Cove Is a Coven," "Dark Years Offshore," and "Cosmic Woodland Guidance" appear on the album *Pine*, a musical collaboration between Ice Tha One and Junia-T. I recorded the poems with producer Junia-T at It's OK Studios at 468 Queen Street West in Toronto, Ontario, on September 12, 2024.

"Tender Was the Night" is partially inspired by the lovers ritual Henry and Marie Clews created for their spirits to meet one hundred years after their deaths at Le Château de La Napoule in Mandelieu-la-Napoule, France.

"Generations Meet in Epwikek" is a poem for my community of No'kmaq Village/Flat Bay First Nation.

"Living and Dying Amongst the Tides" is inspired by AV Poesia, a poetry, photography, and sound-recording website by Stéphanie Filion (translated from French into English by Rachel McCrum). Written/collaged at Rita Joe Indigenous Writers' Retreat at Jampolis Cottage in Avonport, Nova Scotia, on the Bay of Fundy in Winter 2024.

"Watermother" references Daze Jefferies's *watermother* (2023), animation (still), which is part of the exhibition *Stay Here Stay How Stay*, curated by Emily Critch, at the Rooms Provincial Art Gallery in St. John's, Newfoundland, in Winter 2024.

ACKNOWLEDGEMENTS

Wela'lioq to my co-publishers, editor, copy editor, and book designer for all your craft, care, and time spent rewilding together. And for the many trees sacrificed to become this very book you hold in your hands.

I would like to acknowledge my ancestors, both my Mi'kmaq and settler kin and world views. I am grateful and continuously learning from the gifts and teachings of Two-Eyed Seeing.

I would like to thank the ancient lands and crystal waters, seedlings and trade winds that have helped create this collection.

From the lava fields and fjords of Iceland to the gentle breeze and bird-of-paradise blooms on the French Riviera, *Re: Wild Her* began as a way to heal, but has become my raison d'être. This book flies above it all and dances with the earth and sea, and marks the birth of a new way of being.

I am grateful to the muses—real, authentic, and reimagined—for their joie de vivre. To rugged beauty, wild energies, deep undercurrents of love, every dip, divine interventions, my mother, botanicals, No'kmaq Village, wildflowers, tarot decks, omens, weeds, birdsongs, Mi'kma'ki, yoga, Centre Pompidou, tuckamore, E. E. Cummings, seamaids, Paris, my shipmates, Astrud Gilberto, Atlantic Vernacular, Cuba, my grandmothers, Stan Getz, Mexico, the Parcelles, Feist, Cacouna, fishermen, La Napoule Art Foundation, astrology, Château de La Napoule, Pacific Ocean, Kew Gardens, the Sea Ranch, MoMA, Anaïs Nin, Chocolate Lake, Gertrude Stein, my cousins, Ktaqmkuk, my grandfathers, Virginia Woolf, my sisters, pine, clouds, rough drafts, my brothers, Sylvia Plath, Sable Island, Montréal, flamingos, my nieces and nephews, cenotes, raw lessons, my fathers, Atlantic Ocean, the Elders, Lóla Flórens, witches and healers, Iceland Writers Retreat, my aunts, Palais Garnier, artistic fever dreams, my uncles, spirits, curators, my friends and foes, and the sublime April month I spent swimming off the Côte d'Azur.

And to my love, for painting me on his plane and flying me back home.

PHOTO: SHANNON WEBB-CAMPBELL

SHANNON WEBB-CAMPBELL is of Mi'kmaq and settler heritage and lives in Halifax, Nova Scotia. She is a member of Flat Bay First Nation in Newfoundland and Labrador. Her previous books include *Lunar Tides*, *I Am a Body of Land*, and *Still No Word*, which received Egale Canada's Out in Print Award. Shannon holds a PhD from the University of New Brunswick in English-Creative Writing and is the editor of *Visual Arts News* magazine and *Muskrat Magazine*.

COLOPHON

Manufactured as the first edition of
Re: Wild Her
in the spring of 2025 by Book*hug Press

Edited by Sandra Ridley
Copy-edited by Shannon Whibbs
Proofread by Hazel Millar
Type by Jay Millar
Cover by Tree Abraham

Printed in Canada

bookhugpress.ca